# Clifford
## THE BIG RED DOG®

For the real Emily Elizabeth

First published by Scholastic Inc. ISBN 0-590-87957-X
This edition published by Scholastic At Home
90 Old Sherman Turnpike, Danbury, Connecticut  06816.

ISBN 0-439-52203-X

Printed in the U.S.A.

Visit Scholastic.com for information about our books and authors online.

# Clifford
# THE BIG RED DOG®

**Story and pictures by Norman Bridwell**

SCHOLASTIC INC.

New York   Toronto   London   Auckland   Sydney
Mexico City   New Delhi   Hong Kong   Buenos Aires

I'm Emily Elizabeth,

and I have a dog.

My dog is a big red dog.

Other kids I know have dogs, too.

Some are big dogs.

And some are red dogs.

But I have the biggest, reddest dog on our street.

This is my dog—Clifford.

We have fun together. We play games.

I throw a stick, and he
brings it back to me.

He makes mistakes sometimes.

We play hide-and-seek.

I'm a good hide-and-seek player.

I can find Clifford,
no matter where he hides.

We play camping out,

and I don't need a tent.

He can do tricks, too.

He can sit up and beg.

Oh, I know he's not perfect.

He has *some* bad habits.

He runs after cars.

He catches some of them.

He runs after cats, too.

We don't go to the zoo anymore.

He digs up flowers.

Clifford loves to chew shoes.

It's not easy to keep Clifford.

He eats and drinks a lot.

His house was a problem, too.

But he's a very good watchdog.

The bad boys don't come around anymore.

One day I gave Clifford a bath.

And I combed his hair,
and took him to the dog show.

I'd like to say Clifford won first prize.

But he didn't.

I don't care.

You can keep all your small dogs.

You can keep all your black,

white, brown, and spotted dogs.

I'll keep Clifford . . . . Wouldn't you?